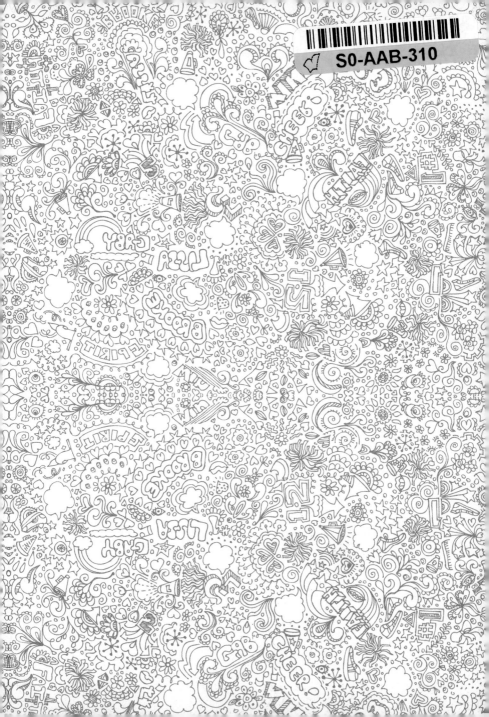

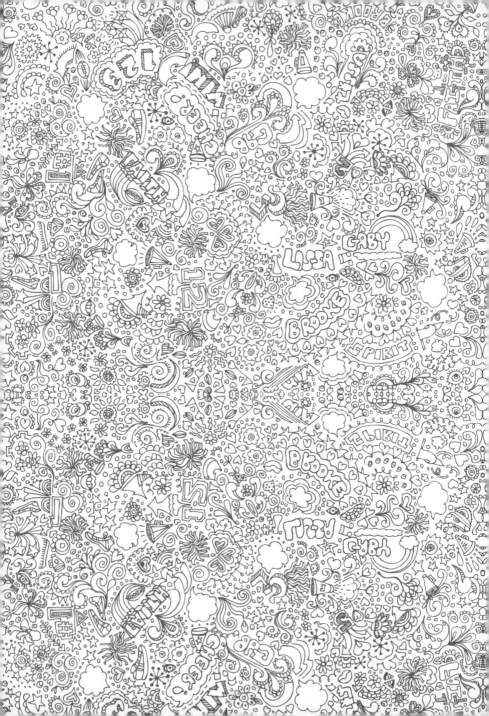

Team Cheer

Faith and the DANCE DRAMA

Team Cheer is published by Stone Arch Books
A Capstone Imprint
1710 Roe Crest Drive
North Mankato, Minnesota 56003
www.capstonepub.com

Library of Congress Cataloging-in-Publication Data
Jones, Jen.
 Faith and the dance drama / by Jen Jones; illustrated by Liz Adams.
  p. cm. — (Team cheer; #5)
 Summary: Even after six months shy Faith Higgins still feels like the new girl on the Greenview cheerleading squad, and the upcoming school dance is making her feel even more awkward.
  ISBN 978-1-4342-4033-0 (library binding)
 1. Cheerleading—Juvenile fiction. 2. Dating (Social customs)—Juvenile fiction. 3. Bashfulness—Juvenile fiction. 4. Best friends—Juvenile fiction. [1. Cheerleading—Fiction. 2. Dating (Social customs)—Fiction. 3. Bashfulness—Fiction. 4. Best friends—Fiction. 5. Friendship—Fiction.] I. Adams, Liz, ill. II. Title.

PZ7.J720311Fal 2012
813.6—dc23   2012000052

Cover Illustrations: Liz Adams
Artistic Elements: Shutterstock: belle,
blue67design, Nebojsa I, notkoo
Cheer Pattern: Sandy D'Antonio

Printed in the United States of America in Stevens Point, Wisconsin.
 032012   006678WZF12

Faith and the DANCE DRAMA

by Jen Jones

STONE ARCH BOOKS
a capstone imprint

Greenview Middle School Cheer Team Roster

NAME	GRADE
Britt Bolton	7th
Kate Ellis	7th
Gaby Fuller	8th
Sheena Hays	8th
Faith Higgins	8th
Ella Jenkins	8th

That's me! Faith Higgins, squad shy girl.

Ella is the squad rich girl who feels best when she can put the rest of us down. But I've got to admit, the girl can cheer. She's one of the best on the squad.

My bestie Gaby is a real cutie! She's bubbly, flirty, and funny. If only some of her could rub off on me.

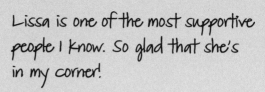

Lissa is one of the most supportive people I know. So glad that she's in my corner!

Ella's sidekick . . . need I say more?

Kacey Kosir	8th
Melissa "Lissa" Marks	8th
Trina Mathews	8th
Brooke Perrino	8th
Mackenzie Potz	7th
Maddie Todd	7th

Coach: Bernadette Adkins

Brooke likes being in charge, and she's good at it, too. But the best thing about her is that she will bend over backward to help you.

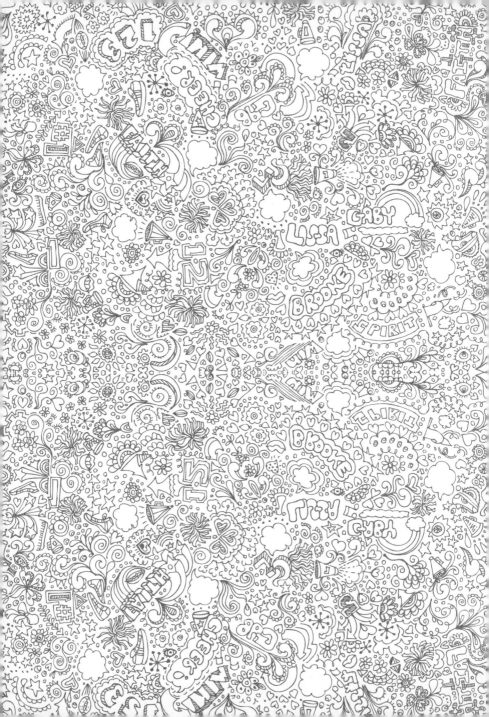

Chapter 1

"Your mom has the coolest clothes!" said Gaby. She sifted through my mom's walk-in closet. She and my other friends were keeping me company while I babysat my brother, Stevie. My parents had gone to see a movie. (Well, if you can call a global warming documentary a movie. Personally, I'd rather cozy up for DVD night with *The Notebook**.) Since Stevie

---

* My mom and I love to watch <u>The Notebook</u>. (It's our go-to movie for our girls' nights, when Dad and Stevie are off doing boy things.) We always squeal when Ryan Gosling comes on screen. Best romance ever!

had already hit the hay for the night, the girls and I were having some fun raiding my mom's closet.

"I kind of dig this tee," said Lissa. She held up a shirt that read "A woman without a man is like a fish without a bicycle." She added a little fist pump for emphasis. "Girl power!"

I just smiled and shook my head. The T-shirt was a perfect example of my parents' hippie tendencies. My mom owned a green interior design firm, which meant she helped other people transform their homes and offices to be more eco-friendly. She met my dad at a protest back in college. Apparently it was love at first picket sign! Too cute.

"What does that even mean anyway?" asked Gaby. She started twirling around in one of my mom's beaded shawls, earning a playful swat from Brooke.

"I think it's a feminist thing," explained Brooke. "Isn't that an old quote from **Gloria Steinem***?" Brooke always knew

---

* After Brooke told me more about Gloria Steinem, I chose her for a biography project at school. Good old Gloria fought for women's rights as a journalist and activist. She also worked for civil rights for minorities.

CALLING ALL GREEN TEENS

ECO TIPS!

With my green mom, it isn't surprising that she's always passing green tips along to me. Here are a few good ones:

1. When you're done with your computer at night, shut it off. (It will save major electricity!)

2. Get involved and join your school's green club. Don't have one? Then start your own!

3. Be a vegetarian at least one day a week. Meat production takes a huge toll on the environment. Cutting back on meat isn't just good for Earth — it's good for you, too!

4. Skip the bottled water and use your own stylish water bottle.

5. Buy digital music! It helps cut the waste that comes from producing and shipping CDs and cases.

random stuff like that. No need to use Google when she was around!

Gaby draped the shawl over her head and made faces in the mirror. "Good ol' Glo may have been on to something," she said. "After all, my brothers do drive me crazy sometimes! But Matt, well . . . he's another story." Matt was one of her brother Tyson's friends and soccer teammates, and she had a super-sized crush on him.

"Mmm, yes, he gets a free pass — that boy is truly *caliente**," said Lissa, who loved to sprinkle Spanish expressions into her everyday English.

"Soccer players are the cutest for sure," agreed Brooke, reaching for her bowl of vanilla gelato. "Too bad we only get to cheer for football and basketball!"

As varsity cheerleaders for Greenview Middle School, we focused mostly on the major sports, as well as preparing for our own cheer competitions. It would be nearly impossible

---

* caliente = hot, as in "Gaby is sure to notice every caliente guy in the room."

to fit in yet *another* team's schedule. But we couldn't help but wish that we could cheer for wrestling, soccer, and baseball! I wasn't really into the "scenery" the way Gaby and some of my other friends were, though. It wasn't that I didn't notice guys, but I tended to keep to myself.

"Well, maybe we can snag a few soccer boys for the dance committee," said Gaby. "We've got tons to do over the next few weeks!"

"Yeah, like raise lots of moolah for Regionals," said Lissa. Our squad had recently placed second at qualifiers. We were proud of our finish, but we wouldn't be receiving a paid bid to the upcoming Regionals. As our squad's fund-raising chair, Lissa was kind of the budget babysitter. She always had money on the mind!

The fall dance was a big deal and a lot of work for the Viking cheer squad. Most of the proceeds went to the athletic department and were divided among the sports. The cheer squad always headed up the committee. People from all the different sports teams helped out. Since this was my first year at Greenview, I could barely wait to see what it was all like!

"What's the theme going to be?" I asked, getting excited.

"Gabs and I are supposed to pick one with Coach A before the first committee meeting," said Brooke. She and Gaby were co-captains, so they often met with Coach Adkins, our fearless (and sometimes fear-inducing!) leader. As a result, they were always in the know about everything.

Gaby suddenly looked guilty. "Um, I kind of borrowed Coach A's notebook so we could sneak a peek at some of the ideas people submitted," she confessed with a grin. She pulled a spiral-bound notepad out of her backpack.

Lissa gasped in mock horror. "Naughty, naughty! But tell us more," she joked, slurping down the last of her gelato.

Brooke snatched the notebook from Gaby, curious to see the list. "Hmm, somebody suggested a *Pirates of the Caribbean* theme," she said. "That could be kind of tropi-cool! I can picture the décor now."

"Maybe, but all the guys would wear fake beards and bandannas — not the best look," Gaby said, laughing. "I'm pretty sure **Johnny Depp*** is the only one who could pull that off. Do we have enough money in the budget for a Jack Sparrow cameo?"

Dance Theme Ideas

- Pirates of the Caribbean
- Millionaires' Masquerade
- CandyLand
- Black and White Ball
- Passport to Old Hollywood
- Crystal Casino
- Hillbilly Hoedown
- Monster Mash
- Alice in Wonderland
- '80s Prom

"I *wish*. Far from it!" said Lissa, reading over Brooke's shoulder. "Ugh, speaking of rich people, looks like *Ella* wants to do Millionaires' Masquerade. No shocker there."

There was no love lost between Lissa and Ella, who could be pretty, well, prissy most of the time. Feisty, down-to-earth Lissa had about zero patience for her antics. Ella

---

* I'm not sure if it's his gorgeous eyes or his amazing acting skills, but Gaby is right. Johnny Depp carries off that ratty pirate beard better than anyone else could.

and I had certainly experienced our own ups and downs over the summer, but once I got used to her, her attitude was a lot easier to take!

Curious, I leaned over to look at the list myself. Some of the ideas were pretty creative. I decided to throw my favorite out to the peanut gallery. "What about this one, 'Passport to Old Hollywood?'" I asked, pointing at the entry.

"Oooh, I likey," said Gaby. "I'm picturing boas for the ladies and dapper looks for the dudes. People with dates could even dress as famous movie couples!"

"Yeah, that's definitely a contender, Faith," agreed Brooke. "Good pick!" She made a star by it in Coach A's notebook, then quickly erased it, realizing that we weren't supposed to have the notebook in the first place.

I grinned, feeling content. Gaby, Brooke, and Lissa had quickly become my closest friends since my family moved to Greenview earlier this year. Being accepted by them always felt really good. Since I was somewhat shy, I hadn't always had an easy time making friends. Cheerleading was definitely helping to bring me out of my sensitive shell.

"Now we just have to find our leading men to take us to the dance!" said Gaby, batting her eyelashes for effect.

"I think I'll bring Dixon," I said, making a joke about Lissa's pet bulldog. "He's the only man for me. We can recreate the movie *Lassie**."

My fave movie couples!
(Perfect costumes for the dance!)

- Grease's Danny & Sandy
- Dirty Dancing's Baby & Johnny
- Harry Potter's Ron & Hermione
- Spider-Man's Spidey & Mary Jane
- Rocky's Rocky & Adrian
- Aladdin's Jasmine & Aladdin
- The Muppets' Kermit & Miss Piggy
- Twilight's Edward & Bella
- Star Wars' Hans Solo & Princess Leia
- The Sound of Music's Maria & Captain Von Trapp
- Walk the Line's Johnny & June

---

* Star of eleven movies, Lassie is the ultimate dog hero! They say that the character was based on a dog that saved a sailor during World War 1. That's what I call *puppy power!*

"Whatever, Faith! I'm sure the guys will be lining up," answered Gaby.

I raised my eyebrows. I doubted she was right, but the thought alone was a little scary. I may have been poking my head out of the shell lately, but the thought of going on an actual date put me into *shellshock*! For now, I was just going to enjoy a spoonful of chocolate-chip gelato and the company of my brand-new besties.

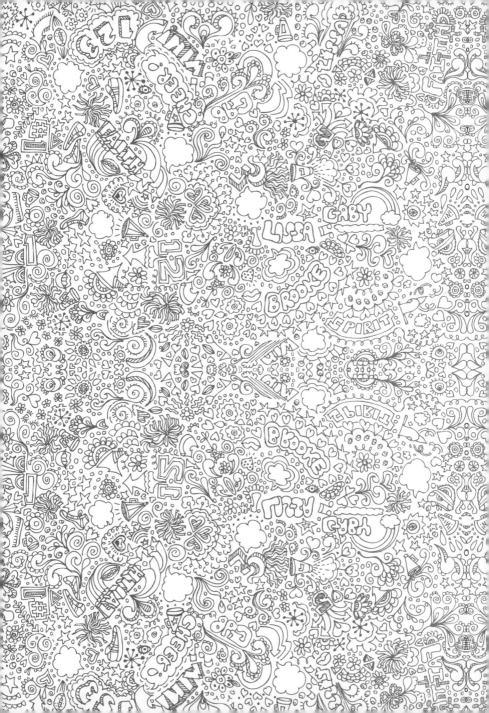

Chapter 2

Gimme a V!
Dot the I
Curl the C
T-O-R-Y

It was our weekly Monday practice, and we triumphantly belted out the final syllables of our newest chant for our audience of one — Coach A. Stationed at the back of the diamond-shaped formation, I hit the last motion with strong arms and a confident nod. (I was always in back, not just because I'm the new girl, but also because I'm really tall.)

Who would have guessed that six months ago I barely knew a **Herkie** from a **hurdler***?

Britt raised her hand. "What do we do on the 'Curl the C' part again?" she asked, and Brooke patiently showed her the move.

"Anyone else have any questions?" yelled Coach Adkins abruptly. "If not, let's work on incorporating the stunt and transition. We have to kick off basketball season with a bang!"

A little chill ran down my spine at the mere reminder of basketball season. I'd finally *just* started to feel at home performing in front of crowds when football season ended about a month ago. Now I'd need to psych myself up all over again to strut my stuff for B-ball!

Before I could get too worked up, Gaby snapped me out of it. "Okay, guys!" she yelled, clapping her hands together.

* Herkie and hurdler are names for two different jumps. In a Herkie, one leg is straight and slightly to the side. The other leg is bent with the knee facing down. The arms vary. A hurdler is similar, but the straight leg is right in front of your face and your bent leg points to the ground — just like you were jumping over a hurdle.

BASKETBALL VS. FOOTBALL

(Why cheering for basketball might feel completely different)

- A basketball court is much smaller than a football field. People are really going to be able to focus in on us. More eyes on me? Yikes!

- Since our voices don't have to compete with the great outdoors, where there is nothing to create echoes, our cheers will seem louder during basketball.

- We can do more decorating for basketball games because we have an entire gym worth of wall to cover with posters!

- We can wear the same uniforms, because we live in a warm climate. But cheerleaders in other parts of the country trade in their football uniforms (pants and hoodies) for new basketball ones (skirts and tanks). It would be crazy to cheer in snow!

"Brooke and I had kind of a light bulb moment. We wanted to run an idea past y'all. What if we spell out the letters using our poms in front while the stunting goes on in back?"

She went on to explain more about the idea, which sounded like an ultra-cool visual effect. I had to give Gaby props. As co-captain, she had really turned out to be a natural leader. In the beginning, Brooke had her doubts about whether the often silly, sometimes spacey Gaby could pull it off. But now there was no doubt she was rocking her role!

Coach A then split us up into two groups so that we could practice more effectively. She was a master at time management! As usual, I was in the stunting group. (Yet another thing that comes along with the tall territory . . . I'm always a base! However, I have no desire to be the center of attention as a flyer, so that's a-okay with me.)

Typically, my stunt group included Brooke, Mackenzie, and Sheena. But for this stunt, we needed *five* girls, so we appointed Trina as another base.

It was a **split extension***, which would feature Brooke doing airborne side splits. Pretty snazzy!

While we practiced hoisting Brooke's legs into position, the remaining seven cheerleaders worked on spelling "V-I-C-T-O-R-Y" with their pom-poms. Gaby and Ella sat down in front, with Lissa, Britt, and Maddie kneeling behind them and Kate and Kacey standing up in back. They had to make a tight cluster so that they could form the letters properly.

"You guys! The poms totally cover up our faces," complained Ella. Unlike me, she did not enjoy going unseen.

Kacey, who always echoed everything Ella said, quickly backed her up. "Yeah, Lissa keeps tickling my nose with her pom when we do the 'T,'" she added, getting the evil eye from Lissa. "I think I'm allergic to metallic plastic!" Kacey did

---

* The split extension was our new BIG stunt. While Brooke did the splits in the air, two bases would each hold one of her legs, and a third base would make sure she didn't over-split. Meanwhile, a fifth girl stands in front of the stunt, holding Brooke's hands. Super impressive!

a dramatic fake sneeze to illustrate her point. She and Ella broke down into peals of laughter.

Before Lissa could fire back one of her trademark comebacks, Gaby stepped in to keep the peace. "Gals, it's only for one verse of the chant! I'm sure you can handle it," she said. "Let's try it again, but this time hit each letter hard and then shimmer your poms."

Brooke and I exchanged a look. We were happy to be on the drama-free side of things! We spent another twenty minutes practicing, and then Coach A ordered us into our positions to run the whole thing full-out.

"**READY?**" called Brooke.

"**SET!**" we answered, launching into the chant.

GIMME A V!
DOT THE I
CURL THE C
T-O-R-Y

After repeating the chant three times with the standard motions, we changed gears for the final verse.

"WHAT'S IT SPELL, VIKINGS?" Brooke yelled.

"VICTORY!" we yelled back with our hands on hips.

"FIRST WE YELLED IT, NOW YOU SPELL IT!" she called to the imaginary crowd. This was our cue to action. As we yelled **"V-I-C-T-O-R-Y!"** we clapped and moved from a V-shaped formation into our assigned groups for the stunt and pom effect. After repeating the yell several times, we lifted Brooke into the splits and she hit a **high V*** on the "Y" for the last pose. The stunt was a little wobbly, but we managed to keep her up!

All of a sudden, we heard whoops and hollers from the corner of the gym. "You go, lady Vikings!" yelled Jack Sullivan, one of the eighth-grade basketball players. Next to him was Micah Robson, and the two of them started doing fake cheerleading moves and cracking up. Off to the side

* High V means that Brooke's arms went up to form a V, with her arms at 1:00 and 11:00.

stood Derek Sowers, who was just smiling and rolling his eyes. I felt my face flush red. They just happened to be, oh, the cutest guys in our class!

"Oh yeah, Robson?" yelled Lissa, grinning. "Try this one on for size." She busted into a **standing back tuck***, followed by a **toe touch**** jump.

Micah made a feeble attempt at a toe touch. "Mmm-hmm, thought so!" Lissa yelled. "Save your hang time for the basketball court, kids."

Not one to take a challenge lightly, Micah grabbed a basketball off the nearby rack and dribbled out onto the court. "You talk a big game, Marks!" he called. "But can you hit this?" He sank an effortless three-pointer, earning applause from Derek and Jack.

—————————

* A standing back tuck is a back flip from the standing position, with the knees tucked in toward the body.

** I was so happy to finally nail a toe touch! It took a while to get my legs fully extended to my sides with my hands reaching toward my toes.

25

"I can't, but I bet our long-and-lean Faith could," said Lissa. "Go represent for the girls, Faith!" She gave me a playful push, but I froze in place. I was *mortified*! It was super embarrassing to be called out for being tall, especially in front of the three hottie Musketeers.

Luckily, Coach Adkins saved the day. "Faith, stay right where you are. We don't have time to waste! Boys, don't you have somewhere to be?" She shooed them away. They headed off to the locker room — throwing out a few more zingers on the way.

Clearly this was going to be a far cry from football season! The football team had always practiced outside on the field, while now we'd have to split practice time in the gym with the B-ball team.

Guess I'd have to adjust to performing for yet *another* type of audience, and this one definitely made me most nervous of all!

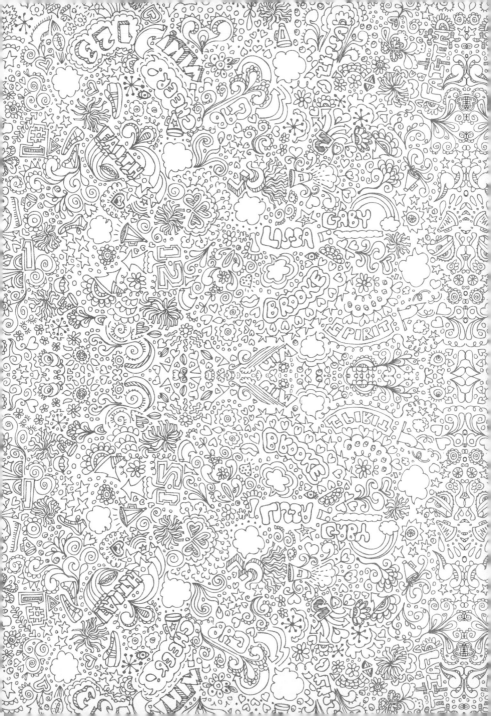

Chapter 3

"Yo, Higgins!" Gaby called across the girls' locker room. "Wanna walk home together? Turns out my class is cancelled." Gaby took dance classes at nearby Groove Studio. She often pirouetted the day away when not cheering for Greenview.

I stuffed my poms inside my cheer bag, pulling out my warm-up jacket with the cursive "G" and my name printed underneath. (I liked that it was starting to get chilly outside. It kind of reminded me of the old days back in Oregon.) "Sounds like a plan, *Fuller*," I joked. She reminded me of Coach A, who always called all of us by our last names.

"Have fun, *chiquitas**," said Lissa, slinging her arm around Brooke's shoulders. "Brooke and I are taking Dixon to the dog park."

"Let's hope he doesn't get all love-struck with that Chihuahua again!" said Brooke, laughing. "And Gabster, don't forget to read chapters three and four of ***Lord of the Rings***** tonight." Brooke tutored Gaby every Monday before practice. She always did her best to keep flighty Gabs on track.

"I'll try, but I'd much rather research dance decorations! If we do Faith's idea of old Hollywood, it'll be kind of like doing my history homework, right?" said Gaby, making a silly face.

~~~~~~~~~

* chiquitas = Spanish for girlfriends, as in "My chiquitas Brooke, Gaby, and Lissa are the best friends around!"

** Every time we begin a new novel, our English teacher likes to give us some extra info on the book and author. J. R. R. Tolkien wrote <u>Lord of the Rings</u> in three volumes over twelve years. It is the second-best-selling book of all time, after <u>A Tale of Two Cities</u> by Charles Dickens.

Mackenzie let out a little snort. She must have overheard the exchange from her nearby locker.

"Whatever you say, girl!" said Brooke. "I need to get an A on the *Lord of the Rings* quiz myself, or else my parents will probably ship me off to an island." When it came to school, her parents had pretty high expectations. But she managed to keep a sense of humor about it most of the time.

After saying *sayonara** to Brooke, Lissa, and the other girls, Gaby and I headed for the home front. We were being cheese balls and skipping down the tree-lined path in front of school when we heard a guy's voice call, "Gaby, Faith, wait up!"

I turned and saw Derek Sowers bounding down the sidewalk. The shyness that I'd felt at practice quickly started to bubble up again. Not that I was some big expert, but in my opinion, he was definitely the best-looking and nicest of all the athletes!

---

* sayonara = Japanese for goodbye

"Derek, what's up?" said Gaby, grabbing his baseball cap and putting it on her own head backward. "I thought you guys had practice."

"We do, but Coach sent me home early," explained Derek. "He wants me to rest my elbow as much as possible so I'm in good shape for the first game." Derek had jammed his elbow in the final football game of the season. So goes the life of a multi-talented athlete!

"Oh yeah, the Vikes need to have our best point guard on point!" said Gaby, poking his side playfully.

"From what I hear, you're not so bad *en pointe* yourself," joked Derek, pretending to do a ballet twirl. He looked at me and added, "I've got a sister in ballet."

As they kept joking around with each other, I started to feel kind of awkward. So *this* was what it felt like to be a third wheel!

Why couldn't I be effortlessly flirty like the Gabster? She somehow managed to be totally charming in just about any

PICTURE THIS!
(Comparing myself with Gaby)

Situation: Three cute boys sit down in front of us at the movies.

Gaby taps one on the shoulder and teases him about being too tall to see over.

I can't wait until the theater goes dark and hope I don't do anything embarrassing before that.

Situation: A couple of boys are kicking around a soccer ball at the park as we walk by.

Gaby tries to steal the ball away, giggling the entire time.

I just keep walking. What do I know about soccer — or boys, for that matter?

Situation: The cutest guy in English says he likes your shoes.

Gaby quickly grins and says, "Thanks! You obviously have great taste. That's an awesome T-shirt."

I turn around looking for these great shoes. Obviously, this compliment wasn't meant for me.

situation. I tended to clam up around people I didn't know very well — especially guys. (Good thing we weren't a coed squad!)

"So, Faith, how do you like Greenview Middle so far?" asked Derek, turning his attention toward me.

My cheeks suddenly felt fiery and I looked away, trying to think of something witty to say. "Oh, um, what's not to like?" I said weakly.

"Your family moved here from Seattle, right?" he asked, making eye contact with me. His green eyes could have rivaled **Rob Pattinson's***!

"Portland, actually," I said, pretending to be really interested in a donut shop sign across the street.

"Yeah, Faith's family is the coolest," chimed in Gaby. "They lived in this really neat open-air house in the woods of Oregon before moving to Greenview."

———~~~~———

* Anyone who knows me knows I LOVE Robert Pattinson. Go Team Edward! Vampires all the way!

"Rad!" said Derek, looking sincerely interested. "So, were you always a cheerleader?"

"No," I answered, trailing off. I made eye contact with Gaby, like, *Save me!* I think I liked it better when I was the invisible third wheel.

She jumped to my rescue. "Can you believe it? This is Faith's first year as a cheerleader. You'd think she'd been a Viking forevs!"

They started talking about basketball season, which gave me a much-needed break from Derek's attentions. We kept walking for a little while, and we finally arrived at Gaby's and my street, Spring Street.

"Well, guess I'll see you guys tomorrow," said Derek, snatching his hat back from Gaby and giving us a sideways grin.

"If you're lucky," said Gaby, fake-grabbing his hat back.

"See ya," I muttered, wishing I could have been more myself during the conversation. It usually took me a while to warm up to people. He gave us a little nod, then sprinted off toward his own neighborhood.

"O. M. Geee!" said Gaby as soon as he was out of earshot. "He was totally all about you, Faith-a-roo!"

"Okay, forget about Derek's elbow. I think the doctor needs to check your head," I said, laughing. The idea was just ridiculous. "I'm like a boring scoop of **vanilla***, and you're colorful Neapolitan. What flavor would *you* pick?"

"Oh, *please*! Derek and I have been friends forever," insisted Gaby. "Besides, I've got my eye on Matt . . . or maybe Micah. Either way, my dance card has an 'M' on it, not a 'D!'"

We approached her house, where her brothers Tyson and Damon were playing hacky sack in the front yard. "Hey, you want to come in for a smoothie? Or maybe some Junior Mints?" asked Gaby. She made no secret of her sweets addiction.

———————

* I shouldn't really get down about being vanilla. After all, it's my grandma's favorite flavor. She says it brings out the best flavors in anything you eat it with. And I try to bring out the best in my friends, too!

"No, I think I'm going to go home and bury my head under my pillow," I said. "Two embarrassing boy encounters in one day? Color me mortified."

"Oh yeah, that was totally hilarious when the guys busted in on practice," remembered Gaby, adjusting her high ponytail. "Guess you'll have to get used to Derek being around!"

I doubted *that* was possible. And I doubted he'd pay me much attention again, anyway. This shy girl had a long way to go before being any sort of boy magnet!

> **Gaby's Famous Smoothie**
> (most people would call it a shake)
> - - - - - - - - - - - - - - - -
> Blend 1 cup each vanilla ice cream, milk, and crumbled chocolate chip cookies with 1/4 cup mini chocolate chips. Top with a cookie.

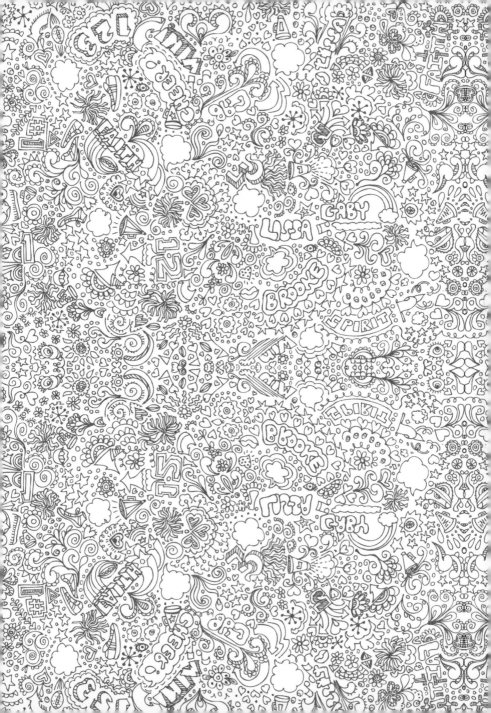

Chapter 4

The rest of the week passed by pretty uneventfully. In other words, no more awkward run-ins with Derek or any other basketball boys! On Tuesday, I helped my mom pick out some paint samples after school, and on Thursday, Lissa and I had a mini-marathon of the ***Bring It On**** movies at her house. But once Friday rolled around, my so-called life suddenly got a *lot* more interesting!

~~~~~~~~~

* Even before I was a cheerleader, I loved the Bring It On movies — obviously! While nothing beats the original, starring Kirsten Dunst and Gabrielle Union as battling captains, the sequels are all really fun too! Maybe someday I'll see Bring It On: The Musical on stage.

The whole thing started out pretty innocently. I was sitting in study hall trying to tackle my science homework when the instant messenger screen lit up.

bpbella: Girl, I have big news. No, scratch that. HUGE news! Are you sitting down?

gottahavefaith: Of course, I'm in study hall at my desk! What else would I be doing? LOL. What's up?

bpbella: Okay, well, spoiler alert: you might be jumping up and down freaking out in about .5 seconds!

gottahavefaith: The curiosity is killing me. Do tell!

bpbella: Here's the scoop: at the student council meeting, I was chatting with Jack Sullivan about the dance. And he said Derek Sowers is going to ask you to be his date!

My heart suddenly skipped about ten beats, and an entire fleet of butterflies unleashed themselves in my stomach. The thought of Derek asking me to the dance was simply the craziest thing I'd heard all day — no, make that all year! I couldn't picture a popular, outgoing guy like him going for a shy social-wallflower type like myself. Clearly, this piece of news couldn't be true . . . could it?

bpbella: Faith? Did I blow your mind? Or are you just busy jumping up and down in glee? LOL

gottahavefaith: I would say #1. Mind is officially blown. Even more than that time we lost to the Panthers in triple overtime.

bpbella: Even more than the time Gaby managed to down five jumbo-sized Hershey bars in ten minutes?

gottahavefaith: Even more than when she finished a strawberry-banana smoothie in one gulp.

bpbella: Wow, that's pretty intense! I have to run, but I'll provide the full rundown later. See you at the committee mtg, and you better start planning what ensemble you're going to rock at the dance!

gottahavefaith: Um, let's wait and see if he asks me first. Otherwise, I'll be all dressed up with nowhere to go. xoxo

Did that really just happen? I pressed "save" on the chat window so that I could make sure this wasn't all just a dream later on. For the rest of study hall, it was almost impossible to concentrate. I kept alternating between daydreaming about going to the dance with Derek . . . and completely freaking out about being asked by him! And all the while, I seriously doubted that the rumor was even true.

Somehow I managed to get through the rest of my classes, but it wasn't easy. Once the bell signaled the end of the school day, I hightailed it toward my locker so I could have a few minutes to breathe and chill before the dance committee meeting. (Cue butterflies again!)

As I headed down the hallway, I could see Gaby and Lissa waiting for me by my locker. So much for my alone time, but I was kind of pumped to fill them in on what Brooke had told me! But it turned out there was no need. They'd already been debriefed by Ms. Perrino herself.

"Faith!" squealed Gaby as I approached. "I told you Derek was into you! Do I know things, or do I know things?"

"I wouldn't go that far," I answered, still in disbelief. "It could just be a rumor. We barely know each other!"

"Maybe he wants another chance to see you do your slam-dunk," teased Lissa. I glared at her playfully. I was *still* annoyed about that whole thing. "So you're going to say yes, right?"

Overwhelmed, I buried my face in my hands. "You guys, I have absolutely zero idea of how to talk to boys. I barely even talked to *girls* until I came to Greenview! Maybe I should just hide in my locker until after the dance." I pretended to climb in, getting a giggle from Faith and Lissa.

"Never fear, young Faith," said Gaby, putting her arm around me protectively. "You have a living, breathing version of *Flirting for Dummies* right here. I'll walk you through everything you need to know!"

"Yeah, if I can tutor you all in Spanish and Brooke can tutor Gabs in English, why can't Gabs can tutor you in boys?" joked Lissa.

The thought was hilarious, but I doubted even Gaby could get me up to speed on everything I needed to know. "The offer is, um, sweet and all, but we better get to the committee meeting before Coach A forms a *search* committee instead!"

Gabs looked at her watch and nodded. "Good call. Fine, I'll give you a crash course while we walk down there. You never know when Derek might do the asking . . . and you need to be ready!"

My head swam as Gaby fired off a seemingly endless list of tips. She definitely seemed to have the art of flirting down! I only wished it was as easy for me.

We were almost to the meeting room when I realized I'd left my notebook in my locker. "Shoot! I've gotta run back," I told Gaby and Lissa. "Save a spot for me?"

Gaby's Flirting Tips

- Don't seem too eager.
- Joke around and bust his chops.
- Smile and make eye contact.
- Stay relaxed, comfortable, and confident.
- Be interested in what he has to say.
- Be yourself!

"You got it, girl!" said Gabs, as I sprinted off toward the eighth-grade hallway again. But I'd barely gotten around the corner before I stopped dead in my tracks. There was Derek, coming down the corridor! And he wasn't alone. He had his arm around another eighth grader, Faith *Moses*, and they were laughing uncontrollably about something.

I quickly ducked into an empty classroom, praying they hadn't seen me. I felt like a total fool! The rumor was obviously about Faith Moses. I should have realized that in the first place. I tried to collect my thoughts, as the butterflies in my stomach transformed into a giant lump. This was way worse than the time we lost to the Panthers in triple overtime.

Panicked at the thought of facing Derek at the meeting, I decided there was no other option but to bail at the last minute. I pulled out my phone and texted Brooke:

Yo B! Turns out my mom needs to pick me up early and I won't be able to make the meeting. Cover for me with Coach A?

She returned my text right away:

On it. Consider yourself covered and I'll call you later.

I felt a little babyish punking out like that, especially since it was likely that Derek didn't even know about the misunderstanding. Plus, I hated lying, and I knew Gaby and Lissa would probably wonder what had happened to me. But I needed the free pass so I could use the afternoon to recover from the disappointment! And from now on, I'd return my focus to school and cheerleading, where it belonged, and leave the guy stuff to everyone else.

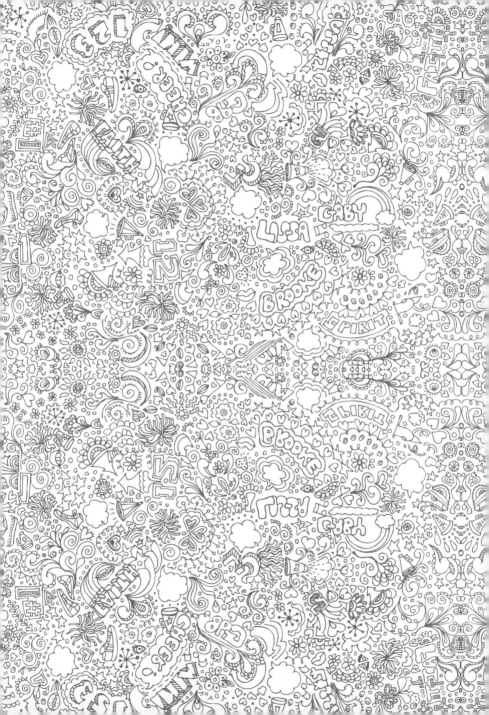

Chapter 5

They say a good night's sleep fixes everything. In this case, let's just say it came pretty darn close! The next morning, I felt way better about the Derek thing and ready to return to the dance committee.

Thanks to a marathon evening phone session, I'd gotten to fill Brooke in. In return, she gave me the full 411 on how the committee meeting went. Sounded like business as usual. Ella had unsuccessfully tried to sway everyone into getting Prada party favors, and Coach A had a mile-long to-do list to assign. The athletes from other teams said their

Dance Committee Meeting: To-Do List

- [ ] Review the date and time for the dance
- [ ] Assign chairs: Who will be in charge of organizing music, decorations, raffle, refreshments, publicity, chaperones?
- [ ] Choose a theme
- [ ] Sign up for times for selling tickets
- [ ] What will we charge for dance tickets? Raffle tickets?
- [ ] Brainstorm ideas for raffle prizes
- [ ] Set up the time for the next meeting

coaches were nothing compared to our drill-sergeant-like diva!

And after debating the theme, they'd finally settled on a final selection. Drumroll, please . . . "Passport to Old Hollywood!" Even though it hadn't been my original idea, it was definitely my fave of the bunch.

It turned out Brooke had some news of her own to share, too. "Okay, I feel bad telling you this after the whole Derek dealio," she said. "But I'm dying to tell someone! Todd Hilson asked me to go today, so I guess I'll have a date that night."

"Brooke, that's awesome!" I exclaimed. And it was. The fact that I didn't have a date didn't mean my friends shouldn't get their guy groove on!

"Thanks," she told me, sounding relieved. "I have to admit, I used to put extra goodies in his candy bag when we made the 'Good Luck' packages for the football team. I've always thought he was a total cutie."

And as for my own former co-star? Being able to confide in Brooke about what happened had helped a lot. The whole thing still stung a little, but I felt like I could return to school with my dignity intact. (Mostly.) I'd just have to stay far, far away from one Mr. Derek Sowers for a while.

When Monday rolled around, I was prepared to move on with style. "Mom, can you help me pick out an outfit today?" I called to my mom. You know how some days you just want to *feel* good? This was definitely one of them. And no one had better taste than my **madre***, as Lissa would put it.

---

* madre = mother, of course, as in "what would I do without my madre to cheer me up on days like today?"

She poked her head into my bedroom a few minutes later. "What about this flirty frock?" she suggested, pulling out a polka-dot minidress after a few minutes of closet browsing.

"I'm not sure 'flirty' is exactly what I'm going for," I said with a frown, sitting down on my bed. "In fact, I feel exactly the opposite."

"Sweetie, I'm sorry you're upset about Derek," said Mom, starting to search for a different outfit.

"I'm not really that upset," I insisted.

As usual, my mom saw right through me. "Then why did you skip the committee meeting?" she inquired.

I started doodling in my notebook. "I just couldn't face him on Friday — the thought was too awful," I admitted. "Brooke practically had to promise my firstborn to Coach A to make up for it. Looks like I'll be stuck selling dance tickets during lunch period today!"

"I think Grandma would get dibs on the firstborn before Coach Adkins," joked my mom, holding up a cute pin-striped blazer and flower pin. "What about this ensemble with some skinny jeans?"

"Ding, ding, ding! We have a winner, folks," I said, getting up to give my mom a giant hug. We topped off the look with my fave red ballet flats and a casual updo courtesy of my mom. She always knew how to make me look — and feel — better!

At lunchtime, I headed out to The Nook for my shift at the ticket table with Gaby and Mackenzie. Ticket prices were set at ten dollars. To raise some additional dough, we'd even snagged some awesome stuff to raffle off. The list of prizes included everything from dance classes

WIN THIS! Raffle Prizes

- Three free classes at Groove Studio
- Gift certificate to The Nook
- Large two-topping pizza at Geno's
- Free pedicure at Nina's Nails
- Skateboard from The Skate Shop
- Greenview hoodie
- Greenview yoga pants
- Greenview headband
- Greenview lanyard

at Groove Studio to spa treatments to Greenview gear like hoodies and yoga pants.

The cheerleaders had all put a lot of time and energy into arranging all the donations and promoting the dance. Even though the proceeds would be split up among Greenview's athletic teams, we figured that the more money raised, the bigger and tastier the cheer squad's piece of the pie would be!

And based on the steady stream of students flowing in, I had high hopes that our efforts wouldn't go unrewarded. Among the familiar faces that stopped by to get tix were Todd Hilson (yay, Brooke!), Gaby's brother Damon, and, of all people, Ella?!

Gaby couldn't resist messing around with her. "Ella, I figured you'd be boycotting the dance," teased Gaby. "After all, we weren't able to snag that Chanel bag as a raffle prize."

"Very funny," said Ella, who seemed to be in a more jovial mood than usual. "It'll be prize enough when Micah Robson says he'll be my date. Can you say, 'hottie-patottie?'"

Gaby's face fell a little. I knew she'd been thinking about Micah as a potential date for herself. Knowing this little tidbit, Mackenzie stepped in. "So you're actually planning on asking *him*?" she asked.

"Of course," said Ella. "I'm a modern woman of the millennium! And, as you can guess, I *love* being in the driver's seat. What about you, Gaby? Who's your date?"

"I don't have one yet," she admitted reluctantly.

Ella patted her shoulder. "Well, you can always stay home and watch movies with Faith," she said, giving me a sly smile. "I'm sure she won't be going!" And with that, she grabbed her two tickets and flounced over to the cafeteria entrance, where Kacey was waiting for her.

I groaned in annoyance. "Ugh! Every time I start to think she's okay, she does something else to bug me," I complained.

"Well, let's prove her wrong!" exclaimed Lissa, who'd dropped by on her lunch break to keep us company. "Who needs guys, anyway? I'd much rather go to the dance and get *loco** with you chicas anyway."

"You're on!" said Gaby, high-fiving her. "Higgins, you in?"

"I'll think about it, pinky swear," I told them, and decided to change the subject back to Ella. Luckily, she was an endless conversation topic! The four of us started trading stories of Ella encounters, one more ridiculous than the next. I was doubled over in laughter listening to Mackenzie remember the time she brought her personal trainer to cheer camp when we were interrupted by a male voice.

"Hey, lunch period's almost up. Is it too late to buy a ticket, or maybe two?"

I looked up and almost doubled over again — but this time in embarrassment! Sure enough, it was Derek. Everyone else smiled and said hello to him, but I just started fishing through a box looking for an imaginary roll of raffle tickets.

———————

* loco = crazy, as in "Nothing is more fun than loco times with my besties!"

"Not at all," said Gaby. "You know we'd stay open a few extra minutes for you anyway, superstar! How many do you need?"

"Well, that depends on if the person I want to ask says yes," said Derek.

My face felt like it caught fire. I was so embarrassed. I didn't want him to know I was crushing on him, especially since he was clearly crushing on the *other* Faith. I tried to summon the quickest excuse I could think of to escape. "Hey guys, can you take care of Derek? I need to get to sixth period early, so I'm going to jam," I said, grabbing my backpack and standing up quickly.

My foot caught on the chair leg and I tripped a little! My face turned even redder, if that was possible. I was a total train wreck. Mackenzie, Gaby, Derek, and Lissa all looked confused. But before anyone could ask me what was up, I just waved and flew out of the cafeteria. I *definitely* didn't have an appetite anymore anyway.

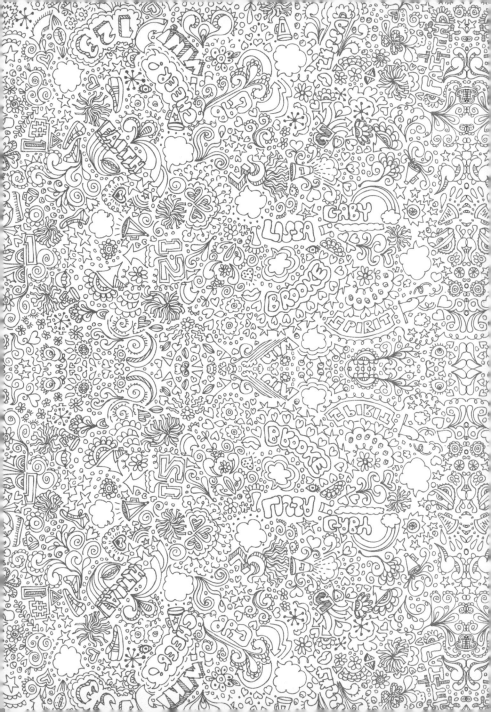

Chapter 6

As we got ready for practice later that day, it was clear that Coach Adkins would definitely have her hands full getting everyone to focus. The whole locker room was buzzing. Everyone was talking about who was asking whom to the dance and what Hollywood looks they'd be rocking! I pretended to be very consumed with lacing up my Asics, hoping to keep to myself for a little while.

No such luck, though, as the girls ambushed me, wanting to know what was up with my mysterious lunchtime exit. "Hey there, Speedy Gonzales!" joked Gaby. "Why the disappearing act earlier? Mackenzie and I had to break down the ticket table all by ourselves."

I felt bad for bailing, but I didn't really feel like going into detail. The whole thing was so embarrassing! Brooke, who was changing into her warm-up suit nearby, caught my eye sympathetically and stepped in.

"I think the *appearance* of Derek may have had a little something to do with Faith's *dis*appearance," she said.

"Why?" asked Gabs. "I mean, he probably never knew you thought he was asking you. No big whoop! Just start over from square one." Oh, Gabs. It was like she had never felt shy or embarrassed in her whole life.

"Easy for you to say," I mumbled. She just didn't get it.

Never one to let people feel sorry for themselves, Lissa tried to lighten the mood. "Faith, just suck it up and come to the dance with me and Gabs," she urged. "It wouldn't be the same without you! You only live once, so you might as well live it up."

I finally managed a real smile. Maybe I was just being silly and overdramatic about this whole Derek thing. After all, the idea of going with a date was really scary anyway. Sure, I'd gotten my hopes up a little with all the hype, but he'd probably done me a *favor* by not asking me. Why not go with my girls and have the best of both worlds?

"Well, when you put it that way, what else can I say, but . . . *sí, senorita**?" I said.

"Now that's what I like to hear. *Muy bueno***!" said Lissa. We started doing a cheesy little do-si-do dance. It felt good to laugh and let loose.

Coach A appeared at the doorway with her whistle. "Move it or lose it, ladies! First basketball game is in less than two weeks, and we've got serious work to do." She left the room with Britt, Maddie, Kate, Trina, and Mackenzie in tow. The rest of us scrambled and followed them.

〜〜〜〜〜

* sí, senorita = yes, miss

** muy bueno = very good, as in "The dance will be muy bueno, even if I don't have a date!"

Once settled into the pre-practice stretch session, we were able to resume the conversation. It was Sheena's and Kacey's turn to lead the stretch, giving Gaby and Brooke a break from their

Be sure to stretch your . . .
* hamstrings
* hip flexors
* inner thighs
* triceps
* shoulders
* back
* chest
* abdomen

usual duties. (At games and competitions, the co-captains always stretched us out, but otherwise, we all took turns at practice.) And that was a good thing, because I seriously needed to debrief this whole dance scene if I was going to go!

"You guys, I'm totally wigging," I confessed as we all reached forward to touch our toes. "I've never been to a dance before. We didn't even have them at my school in Oregon, which was perfectly fine with me!"

"Don't even stress for a single minute," whispered Brooke, narrowing her eyes to see if Coach A was watching.

Not surprisingly, she doesn't like it when we chitchat during practice. "We'll go shopping for dresses together. It'll be so much fun!"

"Oooh, yeah, Forever 21 is supposed to be having a sale," said Gaby, her eyes lighting up at the mention of shopping.

"Can we also buy me a new personality while I'm at it?" I asked, laughing. "In case you haven't noticed, I completely clam up in certain social situations."

Trina cued us to sit down and do our partner stretches. Gaby grabbed my hands. "Don't worry, Faith, it's not like you're going to be flying solo," she whispered, touching her feet to mine and pulling me forward into a deep spread-eagle stretch. "We're going to be the most ravishing trio this school has even seen! Get your lenses ready, red carpet paparazzi."

I giggled, but actually, that brought to mind a good point. Maybe if I channeled a Hollywood starlet, I'd feel more comfortable making my debut at the dance. I started to daydream about showing up as **Grace Kelly***. Or maybe Baby from *Dirty Dancing***. My pink flare dress would be perfect!

Coach A's bark snapped me out of my dreamy haze. "Okay, Vikes, circle up," she said, motioning for us to join her for a quick meeting.

Once we were all gathered, she turned her attention to Lissa. "Marks, what's the update on fund-raising?" asked Coach. "Hit me."

"We've sold about 75 dance tickets so far. We think we'll get up to at least 250," said Lissa. "Plus, the raffle tickets are going like hotcakes!"

Mackenzie piped in. "We were practically turning 'em away at lunchtime today! Right, Faith?" She looked at me for

~~~~~~

* Can you say icon? Grace Kelly was gorgeous, talented, famous, and stylish. And then, to top it all off, she married a prince!

** My mom actually made me wait until I was 13 to watch the PG-13-rated <u>Dirty Dancing</u>. (She's old school like that.) I've been watching it twice a month ever since my birthday. I still get shivers every time Baby does the big jump into Johnny's arms at the end.

NOVEMBER

1

2

3

8

9 Committee
meeting @ 3:30

10

support, and I nodded with enthusiasm. Coach A didn't really need to know that I hadn't exactly *been* there the whole time!

"That's what I like to hear," said Coach A. She pulled a pen from her visor and made some notes in her ever-present notepad. "And Brooke, what's the timeline like with dance preparations?"

Brooke glanced down at her own notepad. She could be pretty businesslike herself! "The plan is to keep selling tickets up until the day of the dance next Friday," she told us. "We've got two more committee meetings before then. We've also reserved the gym next Thursday night for decorating purposes."

4	5 Committee meeting @ 3:30	6	7
11	12 Decorate for dance starting at 3:30 to ??	13 DANCE!	14

Coach A nodded in approval. "Good work, girls," she said. "Keep it up and we'll be sitting pretty come regionals time! Now let's practice 'Gimme a V.'"

As we hopped up to get into formation, everyone started buzzing excitedly about the dance, regionals, and our first basketball game. We certainly had a lot of exciting stuff coming up! And I was determined to try to enjoy every single second. Derek who?

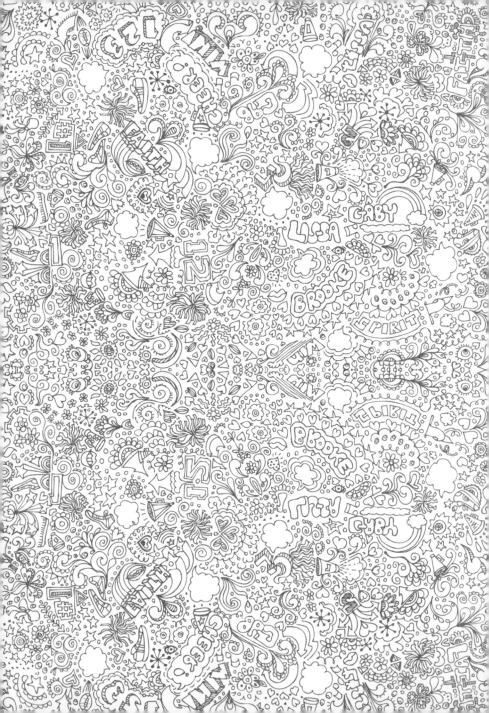

Chapter 7

Homecoming and football season had definitely been a pretty exciting time, but it seemed I hadn't seen anything yet! Greenview was bursting with energy and excitement as the dance and first basketball game drew closer. And even I had finally started to come around. Surprisingly, I was starting to really look forward to it. My first dance! A Kodak moment, indeed.

Luckily, I didn't have too much time to be nervous in the days leading up to the big weekend. There was too much going on! Dress shopping with Brooke, studying for my science test, and dance committee meetings kept me pretty busy. The next week and a half absolutely flew by. It seemed like I'd barely blinked and it was already the day before the dance!

"Move the bleachers over farther," I could hear Coach A barking at the football players. Male and female athletes from all of the different sports teams had gathered to help with dance decorations. A couple hours in and the gym was looking great! Ella and Kacey were busy laying down a red carpet in the entrance with help from some soccer players. Meanwhile, Maddie and Britt were off in a corner hanging the giant "Hollywood" sign we'd all worked on. (Our sign-making skills were coming in pretty handy!)

Party Decor!
It's all in the details

- A red carpet
- Giant Hollywood sign
- Movie star cutouts
- Spotlights
- Feather boas for the girls
- Top hats for the boys

Gaby bounced up to me, draped in strings of pearls. "What should we do with all of these?" she said, twirling one around her finger.

Brooke went into brainstorm mode. "What if we hang them off the light fixtures in the hallway to make them look like chandeliers?"

Gaby beamed, loving the idea. "Now *that's* why you're the brains of this operation, Perrino."

"Yes, but the million-dollar question would be: how do we hang these suckers?" said Brooke. "I can try to find the janitor, but we don't have a ton of time left."

Kate, who was stringing together some lanterns, offered her two cents. "We could do a stunt and hold someone up there," she suggested. "Lift someone up in an **extension*** and let them go to town!"

Brooke giggled. "That's hilarious! That might work, but I'm afraid the person still wouldn't be able to reach. Too bad

* In an extension, the flyer stands with her feet in the hands of the bases, who have their arms fully extended above their heads.

we can't do a two-high stunt," she said, referring to a type of stunt that was illegal except for college-level squads.

"*Unless* we use someone really tall as a flyer," said Gaby, trailing off and mischievously looking my way.

Suddenly the light bulb came on and everyone said together, "Faith!"

Everyone looked at me. I grinned hesitantly. "Well, anything for the team, I guess."

Before I knew it, I was about five feet in the air, perched in the hands of Mackenzie, Sheena, Kate, and Brooke. Lissa stood down below, handing me strands of pearls as we went along.

It was kind of tricky trying to balance and hang stuff at the same time, especially since I'd never flown before. But soon enough, I'd gotten the hang of it. We made four chandeliers, thanks to a healthy amount of teamwork and patience. I was making the final one when I heard a familiar voice down below.

"Pretty impressive! A girl who's hot and handy? I could get used to this," joked Derek, who'd been helping inside the gym. All of the other girls giggled, but I suddenly became very intent on tying the last strand. Why was he *always* showing up at the worst time?!

The girls cradled me out of the stunt and onto solid ground. I frantically tried to cook up an escape plan. Sure, I'd pretty much made peace with the situation, but I still didn't like the face-to-face reminder of it!

Gaby read the panic on my face and took the reins. "Hey D!" she said. "Where were you five minutes ago when we needed some manpower?"

I couldn't help but eavesdrop a little. "I'm pretty sure I was using that manpower to move two tons of bleachers," he said, laughing. "Your coach is no joke."

I tried to concentrate on talking to Sheena, but I had to smile at the thought of Coach A intimidating the burly football players.

"Tell me about it," I heard Brooke chime in. "You guys should start joining us for practice. She'd whip you into shape in no time!"

"Now there's a scary thought," he said. "Speaking of that, I should probably get back to the gym before she hunts me down. You would think this dance was the Oscars or something!" The butterflies fluttered in my stomach again at his mention of the dance. There was still a tiny part of me that wished things had turned out differently.

He took off toward the gym, and Sheena waved her fingers in front of my face. "Earth to Faith! Come in, Higgins!"

I gave her a "sorry" look and forced myself to snap out of it. After all, a certain boy Viking had no place in this earthling's orbit!

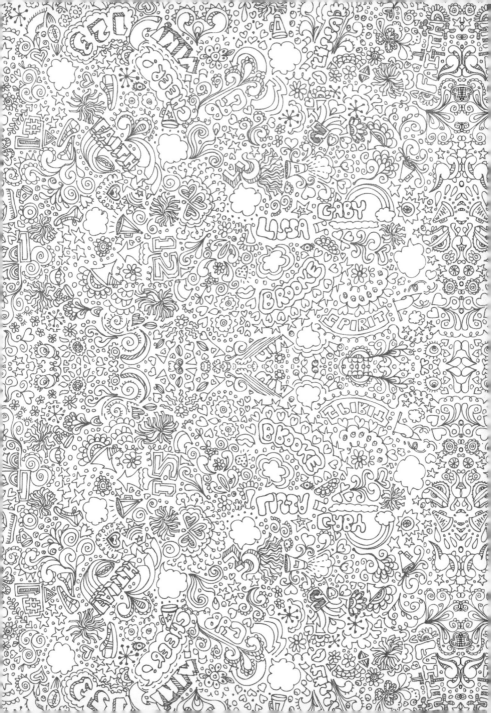

Chapter 8

"Okay, how do I look?" asked Gaby. She modeled her fringed flapper frock in the mirror, correcting a wayward pin curl near her forehead. "Will my new nickname be **Gaby Garbo*** after tonight?"

"You're a starlet for sure," I told her. "Too bad Micah won't be here to see it!" As it turned out, Micah had turned

---

* Gaby was referring to movie star Greta Garbo, an old Hollywood actress we discovered while researching ideas for the dance. Greta made 28 movies from 1922 to 1941, and in 1954, Guinness World Records named her "the most beautiful woman that ever lived."

Ella down and decided to do his own thing for tonight. Maybe I wasn't the only one who wasn't totally ready to dive into the dating pool? That was a comforting thought.

"Micah, shmicah," said Gaby, putting her arm around Lissa's shoulders. "I've already got two hot dates anyway, and one of their names rhymes with Kissa." She gave Lissa a giant smooch on the cheek.

"Aww, thanks, Gabs, but you should probably save your smooches for Matt," said Lissa, wiping a smear of red lipstick off her cheek. "Aren't you going to be seeing him soon?"

"Yeah, we're going to go for ice cream after the basketball game tomorrow," Gaby said, beaming. "Maybe I should have asked him to be my date to the dance. But Tyson didn't think he'd want to be bothered with some measly junior high dance." Matt was in the ninth grade at Greenview High.

"I doubt that, but I'm glad we get you instead," said Lissa, as Brooke re-entered my room from the bathroom. She looked amazing! She and Todd had decided to go as Scarlett O'Hara and Rhett Butler from *Gone with the Wind**. She wore a flowy, full white dress with a red belt and had her hair in long loose curls. "Brooke, you look gorgeous!" I told her, admiring the ensemble.

"I do declare," she said in a Southern-belle accent, curtsying for effect. "I hope Todd feels the same way. And I must say, all of you guys look positively red-carpet-ready yourself!"

Not to toot my own horn, but we did look pretty cute! Lissa was channeling **Audrey Hepburn****, rocking a little black dress and smart updo with her dark hair piled high in a bun. I'd decided on the *Dirty Dancing* look, so I was wearing

---

* Brooke loves being dramatic, and you can't get much more dramatic than Scarlett O'Hara from Gone with the wind. The Civil War combined with a rocky love story makes for lots of DRAMA!

** Lissa's get-up was inspired by Audrey Hepburn's look in a 1961 movie called Breakfast at Tiffany's. You might recognize it as the movie Blair Waldorf is obsessed with in Gossip Girl.

my pink flare dress and had my hair curled pageboy style. I started to wonder what Derek and the other Faith were wearing, but quickly squashed the thought. Nobody would put this "Baby" in a corner tonight! Or at least that's what I was trying to tell myself.

"Faith, are you guys almost ready?" called my dad. "I want to take some pictures in the front yard before Todd and his dad get here." Brooke had arranged for Todd to pick her up here since she didn't want to miss out on primping with us!

"We'll be down in a sec!" I yelled.

"Well, make it snappy!" said my dad.

Getting Ready!

- ☐ Shower, soak, and shave
- ☐ Apply deodorant
- ☐ Paint nails and toenails
- ☐ Lotion up
- ☐ Wash face & brush teeth
- ☐ Apply makeup—but not too much
- ☐ Get dressed, and be sure to accessorize
- ☐ Do hair
- ☐ Pack purse: a lip gloss, mints, a little money, and dance ticket

I groaned and turned back to Brooke, Lissa, and Gaby. "Well, what do you think, gals? Should we step out in style?"

"No day like today," sang Gaby, singing a line from one of our fave musicals, **Rent***.

We headed outside to meet my dad, who'd already set up his Nikon on the tripod. He lived for stuff like this! My mom stopped me at the door, looking a little teary. We were sappy like that.

"Honey, I'm so excited for you," she said, drawing me close. "Enjoy every second tonight, and don't be nervous. You'll have an awesome time."

"Weirdly, I'm not all that nervous for once," I told her, and strangely, it was true. Maybe having my friends as a support system was more powerful than I thought! "Now I can cross 'Go to a school dance' off my bucket list." The bucket list was a running joke in our family.

---

* My BFFs and I aren't just fans of cheerleading movies. We love musicals, like _Rent_, too! After all, the dancing gives us lots of choreography ideas.

"C'mon, Faith, it's time for your close-up!" joked Brooke. She, Lissa, and Gaby were already lined up on the lawn, posing for pics.

I paused for a second, just taking in the moment. A year ago, I'd been in a totally different city with totally different friends. (And not many of them, at that.) Cheerleading wasn't ever something I thought I'd do. What a difference a year makes! And, judging by the look on my mom's face, she was marveling at the dramatic change as well.

My dad took a bunch of pictures, with us mugging and being silly in most of them. Lissa, Gaby, and I did a few *Charlie's Angels**-style poses, and the four of us even did a mini-stunt in our dresses!

Our photo shoot was such a blast that I barely processed the fact that I'd have to see Derek and Faith once I got to the dance. But when Todd's dad's Audi pulled into the driveway,

* <u>Charlie's Angels</u> . . . three girl crime fighters who always look good. They are so entertaining that it is no wonder that Hollywood types keep bringing them back in new movies and TV shows.

the butterflies returned in full force! Maybe I was just a teensy bit nervous after all.

Todd got out of the car, looking adorably Rhett Butler. He gave a beaming Brooke a big hug and presented her with a corsage, earning an "Aww!" from all of us. My mom made eye contact with me, and I could tell she was picturing the day when I'd have a date of my own.

"Let's get a group shot," said my dad. We all lined up, and the butterflies in my stomach went into overdrive again as the night officially began.

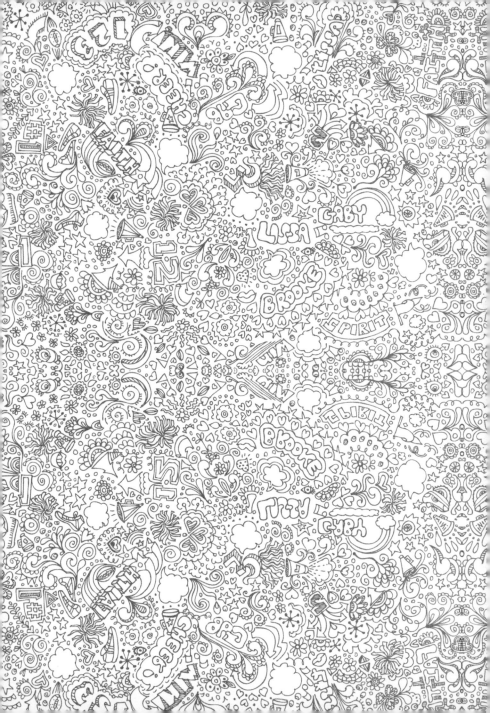

Chapter 9

"Last chance to get raffle tickets!" called Scott Masterson,
a baseball player who was stationed outside in a last-ditch
effort to raise more money. The entrance looked amazing.
We'd strung lanterns between the pillars, and the red carpet
spilled out of the doorway down the exterior steps. If this was
what *middle* school dances were like, I couldn't wait to get to
Greenview High!

Britt and Jean greeted us once our group made it inside.
They'd offered to work the ticket table for the first half of the
night. "Welcome to Hollywood!" they said jokingly.

Lissa handed Britt our tickets, which were designed like a passport. Britt stamped them with a graphic of the Hollywood sign to show that we'd paid the entry fee! I thought it was a pretty creative way to do the ticketing, and I was proud of Gaby for coming up with it.

Inside the gym, lights were flashing and lots of kids were already on the dance floor grooving out to a **Kanye West*** song. Not exactly old Hollywood, but hey, a good tune is a good tune! I spotted Coach A and a few other chaperones over by the drink table, and I also noticed Ella on the dance floor with a mystery man. It appeared Micah was already old news.

Even though it was exciting, I felt a little panicked now that we were here. What were we supposed to do? Dance? Sit around and talk? Get a snack? I wasn't exactly a pro at this. Luckily, Gaby took the guesswork out of it. She threaded

* Hip-hop star Kanye West is all over cheer-competition routines. "All of the Lights," "Stronger," and "Golddigger" are some of the best tunes to choreograph to.

her arms through mine and Lissa's and led us onto the dance floor to join Trina and some others.

It was really fun seeing all the costumes. I spotted a *Pretty Woman* look-alike who was a dead ringer for Julia Roberts, Cinderella and Prince Charming, and lots of other Hollywood faves. And yes, there was also Derek, who was dressed as Danny Zuko from **Grease***. But Faith Moses was nowhere to be seen! Maybe she was in the bathroom fixing her Sandy costume?

A few songs later, we were booty-shaking to Beyonce when I felt a tap on the shoulder. I turned around. It was Danny — I mean Derek!

"Hey, Faith," he said, toying nervously with the collar of his leather jacket. "Can I talk to you for a sec?"

There was no escape route this time. I had to face the music. "Um, sure," I said, following him over to the bleachers.

---

* Of course, Derek would have to come dressed as Danny from Grease. It just happens to be one of my all-time favorite movies! You can't beat a musical set in the 1950s. Olivia Newton-John has the sweetest singing voice, and John Travolta has the best dance moves.

As we sat down, I felt thoroughly confused and decided to let him do the talking. "What's up?" I asked.

"Well, I just wanted a chance to actually talk to you!" he said. "You definitely don't make it easy."

I felt tongue-tied and wasn't sure what to say. (Surprise, surprise!)

"I know, I'm sorry," I admitted. I realized he might misinterpret my shyness for being unfriendly. "I'm kind of on the shy side."

"I wondered about that," he said. "Ever since that day we walked home together, you've acted like you wanted nothing to do with me! But I guess I like a challenge. I've been trying to ask you to the dance all week."

What? Was he for real? I could see Gaby and Lissa watching from afar, and I wondered if this was a practical joke or something.

"Me?" I asked, still confused. "I thought you wanted to take Faith Moses."

"Faith? No way! She and I have been friends since kindergarten. She's practically like a sister," said Derek, wrinkling his nose. "So *that* explains why you've been avoiding me!"

I had no words. I was beyond shocked! He really had wanted to ask me? This was insane! "Can you forgive me for being a total snob?" I asked finally, feeling really silly.

"Sure, I *suppose*," said Derek jokingly.

Fueled by adrenaline, I decided to do something totally out of character. It was a "What would Gaby say?" kind of moment. "In that case, I challenge you to a dance-off! I just might even let you win," I said.

"You are so on," said Derek, taking my hand (!) and leading me down the bleachers toward the dance floor. But right as we got down there, the rap song that was playing switched to a slow song. I was pretty sure it was "Moon River" from *Breakfast at Tiffany's*, but I'd have to ask Lissa later if I was right.

I had absolutely no idea how to slow dance, so I shot a quick look at some other couples to learn what to do. Brooke had her arms around Todd's neck and her head on his shoulder, so I decided to mimic her moves to be on the safe side. Derek put his arms low around my waist. We started swaying back and forth to the song. I had the same "pinch me" feeling I'd had when I saved the original chat transcript from Brooke. Was this *really* happening? Unbelievable.

"I'd really like to get to know you better, Faith," said Derek, pulling me a little closer. I detected the faint smell of cologne on his neck, which was nice.

"Me, too," I told him. And I meant it . . . times 100! Maybe boys weren't the mysterious, unattainable characters I'd made them out to be! Progress. Looking up at the bleachers, I saw Gaby and Lissa giving me thumbs-up signs. We'd have a lot to discuss later on.

Ella waltzed by us with a tall guy I recognized from Greenview High School. I had to hand it to her. She looked breathtaking in a sequined tank dress and peacock feather headband. Everyone looked so fabulous! Why couldn't we dress like this all the time?

"I'm so done with middle school boys," Ella whispered in my ear. "But I can see why they'd be okay for you. You guys actually look cute together!" It was a backhanded compliment, but I'd take it—especially from Ella!

We danced to a few more songs, and then Derek excused himself to go say hi to some friends. I decided to take advantage of the time to go find my girls! Gaby and Lissa were by the drink table, grooving out to the Katy Perry song playing loudly over the speakers.

Hey DJ, Play This Song

- "Vogue" by Madonna
- "Girls Just Want to Have Fun" by Cyndi Lauper
- "Hey Ya" by Outkast
- "Crazy in Love" by Beyonce
- "Thriller" by Michael Jackson
- "I Will Survive" by Gloria Gaynor
- "Yeah" by Usher
- "Tik Tok" by Ke$ha
- "YMCA" by Village People
- "Bad Romance" by Lady Gaga
- "California Girls" by Katy Perry

"California girls, they're unforgettable," sang Gaby, bumping hips with me to the beat.

"This whole *night* is unforgettable!" I said, dancing my way into the group of girls they were standing with.

"You can say that again," said Lissa. "What a turn of events! I guess we'll forgive you for ditching us for another date." She stuck her tongue out at me to let me know she was kidding. I just shook my head and grinned, still in shock at what was going on.

"Girl, you are positively glowing," Gaby added. "Cute couple alert! You and Derek are like a match made in Hollywood heaven! His Danny Zuko could pass for your Johnny Castle, Baby. And we are soooo excited for you."

I was super-excited myself. If this was what heaven felt like, I didn't ever want to come back to earth. And after Derek hugged me goodbye later that night, I wondered if my feet would ever touch the ground again!

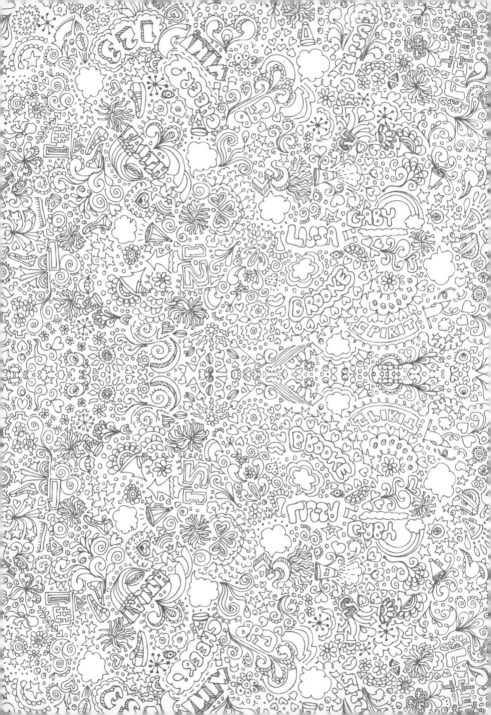

Chapter 10

The dance may have been dunzo, but the weekend was far from over. On Saturday, it was time to regroup for the first basketball game of the season! We had a tradition of decorating the guys' locker room before big games. So we all met at school a few hours early to get it done. Needless to say, we were all pretty pooped from the night before.

"Was it **Naomi Campbell*** who said she doesn't get out of bed for less than $10,000?" groaned Gaby, rubbing her eyes sleepily. "I feel her pain."

---

* I think supermodel Naomi Campbell might be more famous for her divalike behavior than her modeling. She's been accused of violence against people like ten times!

"Deal with it, diva," said Brooke jokingly. "We've got a lot to do, and we still need to run through 'Gimme a V' a few times in the gym after we finish decorating."

"Well, before we do

> **Decorate that locker room!**
>
> - Hang streamers in your school colors
> - Make and hang large posters with upbeat messages
> - Make and hang individual signs for lockers
> - Leave a basket of fruit and granola bars with a good-luck note

that, I need to get the skinny from Faith on last night," said Gaby, turning her attention toward me. "Inquiring minds need to know. Did you get a K-I-S-S?"

As usual, my face flamed up with embarrassment. I couldn't believe she went there in front of everyone! "Oh, uh, no," I told her. "A hug was about as scandalous as things got, and that is perfectly fine with me." I still couldn't believe I'd spent almost the whole night talking and dancing with Derek. Any sort of liplock would have put me over the edge.

"Well, it's never too late," teased Gaby, taping a good-luck poster on one of the guys' lockers. "Maybe you can lay one on him if we win the game."

"*If?*" said Coach A, coming up behind us. "Make that *when*, Fuller. And there'll be no PDA on my watch!"

"Nothing to worry about there, Coach," I said. I was mortified that she'd overheard even a little bit of the conversation.

We raced through the rest of the decorating so that we could sneak in some practice time before the game started. The basketball players had already started warming up in the gym, so we were forced to make do with a tiny area behind the bleachers. We made it work by forming a tighter formation and just marking the moves rather than going **full-out***. I was a little concerned that we weren't able to

---

* When we go full-out, it means we are doing our routine or cheer or whatever exactly as we would in front of a crowd, complete with smiles on our faces. When we mark the moves, we walk through the steps, making sure we hit our counts, but we don't hit every stunt or jump.

practice the split extension with Brooke. But I figured we'd done it enough times in practice that it would probably go off without a hitch! (Fingers crossed, anyway.)

It wasn't long before people started arriving and the basketball team started wrapping things up on the warm-up front. Derek was waiting in line to practice his lay-up one more time. He looked adorable in his blue and red basketball uniform! I wondered if he'd even notice us cheerleaders or if he'd be too in the zone.

As the countdown clock neared zero, we got in position to form our team tunnel for the player introductions. For the tunnel, we stood in two lines facing each other and joined poms up high so that the players could run through.

"Vikings, are you ready to meet your starting lineup?" boomed the announcer. It was our cue to shimmer our poms and the band's cue to start playing the team fight song. The crowd cheered as each guy was announced one by one. They ran out to the floor to take their positions. I could see Derek standing by the bench clapping and cheering on the other guys. I knew it must have been tough for him, since his elbow injury was keeping him somewhat sidelined for now.

"C'mon, Faith, it's almost time for tip-off!" said Mackenzie. She grabbed my arm to lead me over to our space near the cheering section.

Once on the sidelines, we formed a staggered line. Gaby, Trina, Brooke, Lissa, Ella, and Britt were in front. Kacey, Sheena, Mackenzie, Kate, Maddie, and I were in back. It was the same assigned sideline formation we'd used for football season, and it'd worked really well. Why fix things if they aren't broke?

We stood in ready position until Brooke called the first offense chant. (I could hear Coach A's voice in my head: *Hands on hips, smiles on lips!*)

It'd taken me a while to learn all the basketball chants. But I felt pretty confident as Brooke and Gaby took turns leading us through the ones we'd learned. When the other team's coach called timeout, it was time to hit the floor and lead the cheering section in a crowd participation chant.

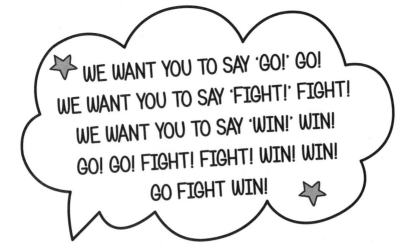

The crowd stomped and clapped as the buzzer sounded, signaling the end of the timeout. I was excited to see that the coach had substituted Derek in for the starting point guard.

"Go, Derek!" I yelled at the top of my lungs, a little embarrassed at how excited I was to see him on the floor. He shot a quick smile my way, causing Brooke and Lissa to giving me knowing looks from the front line.

It was awesome watching Derek do his thing. The first half flew by with the other team leading by six points. As our team ran past us to the locker room, Derek gave me a high-five. I may have been rooting for the whole team, but number 42 was definitely my favorite.

"Ready to do the halftime thang?" asked Gaby, motioning the time to huddle up. "Let's do this!"

We put our hands into the center of the circle. "1-2-3. GO GREENVIEW!"

As we ran out onto the floor, we all started wilding out and doing flips, round-offs, and high kicks. We were psyched to debut the "Gimme a V" routine to the crowd. As it turned out, the crowd loved the way we used our poms to spell the letters in "Victory," and they happily shouted them along with us. When we lifted Brooke into the split extension, they cheered even louder. It felt fantastic! I only wished Derek had been there to see us. The cheer had come a long way since that first practice.

And I'd come a pretty long way myself. I wasn't sure if Derek and I would ever go on a real date, or if I'd ever be totally outgoing the way lots of the other cheerleaders were. But I was open to whatever the future brought . . . and I couldn't wait to see what that would be!

Glossary

ADDICTION (uh-DIK-shuhn)—the state of being unable to give something up

ADRENALINE (uh-DREN-uh-lin)—a chemical produced by your body when you are excited, frightened, or angry

ALLERGIC (uh-LUR-jik)—if you are allergic to something, it causes you to sneeze, get a rash, or have another unpleasant reaction

ALTERNATING (AWL-tur-nayt-ing)—taking turns

AMBUSHED (AM-bushed)—attacked in a surprising way

CONCENTRATE (KON-suhn-trate)—to focus your thoughts and attention on something

EMPHASIS (EM-fuh-siss)—importance given to something

ENSEMBLE (on-SOM-buhl)—a set of clothes that look nice together

HILARIOUS (huh-LAIR-ee-uhss)—very funny

INNOCENTLY (IN-uh-sent-lee)—without guilt

INTERIOR (in-TIHR-ee-ur)—the inside of something

INVISIBLE (in-VIZ-uh-buhl)—unable to be seen

MISINTERPRET (mis-in-TUR-pret)—to understand or explain wrongly

MORTIFIED (MORT-uh-fied)—very embarrassed

POTENTIAL (puh-TEN-shuhl)—possible but not yet actual

SCANDALOUS (SKAN-duhl-us)—shocking or disgraceful

TENDENCIES (TEN-duhn-sees)—leanings toward a particular kind of thought or action

UNATTAINABLE (uhn-uh-TAYN-uh-buhl)—unable to be achieved or reached

Cheer!

Tell me the truth...

Looking back on everything, I wonder if there were better ways to deal with my embarrassment and uncertainty. My nerves were so out of control, I couldn't think straight. How would you have handled these things?

- I felt so awkward walking home with Gaby and Derek. What sort of things could I have talked about? How could I have been a bigger and better part of the conversation?

- When I mistakenly thought Derek wanted to ask Faith Moses to the dance, I felt so awful that I skipped the dance committee meeting. What would you have done in that situation?

- Sometimes being shy can come across as being stuck up. Have you ever been in a situation when extreme shyness was mistaken for a snobbish attitude?

The online forums of my favorite cheer magazines have been my go-to place to post questions about the sport. Some of the questions are about school, friends, and parent stuff. So I can probably answer a question or two. Help me write answers to these great questions!

Why can't my mom leave me alone?
posted 7 hours ago by needSPACE

My mom is constantly asking where I'm going, who else will be there, and when I'll be home, plus she expects me to text her a "check-in" at least once an hour. It is a bit much! How can I get her to back off?

I can't eat with my team!
posted 3 days ago by No-Milk Millie

My squad always wants to go out for pizza after a big win. I can't eat pizza: the cheese makes me sick. I'm too embarrassed to say anything, so I usually skip. But I feel like I'm missing out on bonding time. Help!

Which cheerleader are you?

Quiz: Are you Brooke, Faith, Gaby, or Lissa? Take this fun quiz to find out which cheerleader you're most like.

1. You forget your homework. You:

A. Make sure to talk to the teacher about it privately. You don't want to draw attention to yourself in class.

B. Turn it in the next day, and ask for an opportunity for extra credit so you can make up missed points.

C. Head to the library to tackle it ... again. Looks like you have to redo it in order to get it in on time.

D. Don't realize it until it's time to hand it in, so you make a joke, give a grin, and promise the teacher you'll turn it in tomorrow.

2. The school play is coming up. You:

A. Volunteer to be a stagehand. You like being involved, but you aren't going to get up in front of anyone.

B. Have no plans to try out. You like to stick to physical extracurriculars.

C. Would love to try out, but will it fit into your busy schedule?

D. Plan to try out. After all, you love to meet new people!

3. You have a free afternoon. You:

A. Paint in your room. You like to spend time by yourself to rejuvenate.

B. Head out for a hike. It will be good exercise.

C. Start with some study time, go on a bike ride, and then make plans for the party you are hosting.

D. Work on some new choreography. There are some new dance steps you have been dying to add to the school song routine.

4. Cheerleading tryouts are next week. How do you feel?

A. Uncertain. Cheerleading sounds fun, but the limelight is a little too hot for you.

B. You can't wait. You're going to nail that new tumbling pass.

C. Awesome! After tryouts, you'll be one step closer to becoming captain.

D. Pretty excited . . . you'll be back with your girls, and making new friends, too.

Quiz continues on the next page!

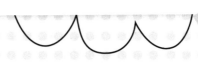

5. Your favorite thing about cheerleading is:

A. Learning a new skill. You had no idea you had it in you.

B. Working toward a common goal, like new uniforms or fees.

C. Helping others learn the cheers and dances so they can do their best.

D. Making posters and goody bags for the teams. It's fun to chat and hang out as we're working.

6. What role do you fill on the squad?

A. New girl — I'm still figuring it out.

B. Treasurer — I can tell you how much money we have (or need).

C. Leader — I like to make sure everyone is in the know.

D. Social butterfly — I see to it that cheerleading is fun for everyone!

7. My family . . .

A. Has a lot of fun coming up with crazy things to do together.

B. Is small, but tight. I can count on my mom for anything.

C. Is proud of me. They encourage me to work hard and be my best.

D. Is loud and fun! It's bound to be, with all those siblings around.

8. When I'm with my friends, you can be sure I:

A. Will be a good listener. And if the moment arises, I'll get a laugh or two.

B. Will tell people exactly what's on my mind. I'm sassy like that.

C. Have organized an activity for us. I like making sure everyone is having fun!

D. Will be happy and carefree. And if someone has a fashion crisis, I'll be solving it.

If you chose:

-----> **Mostly A** — You are Faith. You may be shy, but when you're with your friends or family, you shine with your sweetness and fun sense of humor.

-----> **Mostly B** — You are Lissa. You work hard to meet your goals. Best of all, your friends know they can count on you to be honest and supportive.

-----> **Mostly C** — You are Brooke. You like to be in charge, and you're good at it. If a friend or teammate comes to you, she knows that you'll be happy to help her.

-----> **Mostly D** — You are Gaby. You make friends easily and can be counted on to ease the mood. Friends appreciate your spunky style and sheer silliness.

HOT SHOTS

Game-winning free throws. Amazing three-pointers. Players speeding up and down the court. Basketball season is full of fast-paced fun! And cheerleaders see it all from their prime spot on the sidelines. Follow these tips to get nothing but net.

Take the floor: Halftime and quarter breaks are great times to show your stuff on the court. Short dance routines and chants are sure to keep the crowd pumped as the team recharges.

Keep the energy up: There are few places where spirit runs higher than in a basketball arena. Noise levels skyrocket, fans go crazy, and the team feeds off the energy. It's your job to keep it that way. Encourage the crowd to yell along with you.

Basketball Cheers

Take it to the top, big blue
Push it to the limit X
The [school name] team is really hot
[Team name] gonna win it!

The blue and gray are back X
And better than before X
Get ready for the [team name] heat
As we take the floor!

Basketball Chants

Dribble it X
Just a little bit XX

Remember, X=CLAP

Take that ball away
Defense, take that ball away!

Hit that shot, [team name]
We want a basket

Wildcats X get tough X
Show 'em X your stuff! XX

* Excerpted from *Cheers, Chants, and Signs: Getting the Crowd Going*, by Jen Jones, published by Capstone Press in 2008.

Meet the Author:
Jen Jones

Author Jen Jones brings a true love of cheerleading to her Team Cheer series. Here's what she has to say about the series, cheerleading, and reading.

Q. What is your own cheer experience?

A. I absolutely love cheerleading! I cheered from fifth grade until senior year of high school, and went on to cheer for a semi-pro football team in Chicago for several years. I've also coached numerous teams, and I write for a few cheerleading magazines.

Q. Did any of your family members cheer?

A. Some families are into football — mine is into cheerleading! My mom was a coach for close to 20 years, and my sister cheered throughout grade school and high school. My aunt and cousins were also cheerleaders.

Q. Which cheerleader from the series are you most like?

A. I would say I am probably a combination of Gaby and Brooke: Gaby for her outgoing, bubbly nature, and Brooke for her overachieving, go-getter side. In certain situations, I wish I could channel some of Lissa's feisty fabulousness!

Q. What sort of goals did you have when writing the series?
A. My goals were to create relatable characters that girls couldn't help but like, and also give readers a realistic look at what life on a young competitive cheer squad is like. I want readers to finish the book wanting to be a member of the Greenview Girls!

Q. What kind of reader were you as a kid?
A. I loved to read and often brought home dozens of books every time I went to the library. Whether at the dinner table or in bed, my nose was ALWAYS in a book. Some of my favorite authors were Judy Blume, Lois Duncan, Lois Lowry, Paula Danziger, and Christopher Pike.

Read all of the Team Cheer books!

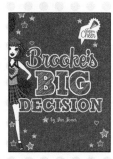

#6-Lissa on the
Sidelines

#7-Save Our
Squad, Gaby

#8-Brooke's Big
Decision

THE FUN DOESN'T STOP HERE!

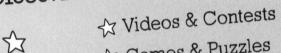

DISCOVER MORE AT WWW.CAPSTONEKIDS.COM

- ☆ Videos & Contests
- ☆ Games & Puzzles
- ☆ Friends & Favorites
- ☆ Authors & Illustrators

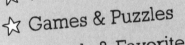
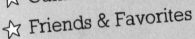
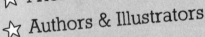

Find cool websites and more books like this one at www.facthound.com. Just type in the Book ID: 9781434240330 and you're ready to go!